TYMES GOE BY TURNES

Stories and poems
for Solstice Shorts 2020

ARACHNE PRESS

First published in UK 2020 by Arachne Press Limited
100 Grierson Road, London SE23 1NX
www.arachnepress.com
© Arachne Press 2020
ISBNs
Print 978-1-913665-18-0
ePub 978-1-913665-19-7
Mobi/kindle 978-1-913665-20-3

Thanks to Arachne Friends: Sarah Lloyd, Maria Kirby, and Catriona Jarvis for their support in making of this book, and to the 29 crowdfund supporters who helped finance the festival.
Thanks to Muireann Grealy for her proofing.
Thanks to Kevin Threlfall for his cover design
Printed on wood-free paper in the UK by TJ International, Padstow.

Acknowledgements

179cm © C L Hearnden, 2020
A Felled Tree © Brooke Stanicki, 2020
a memory forgotten © Sean Carney, 2020
Beach Clean © Ness Owen, 2020
Bringing in the Fruit and *Piano Lessons* © Claire Booker, 2020
Cronos © Laila Sumpton, 2020
Deep Blue Sea © Linda McMullen, 2020
For Ellen © S B Merrow, 2020
In Dark © Karen Ankers, 2020
In the Rocks © Lynn White 2020
New Orleans To Vancouver: A Railway Journey
                                    © Katie Margaret Hall, 2020
Ni de aquí, ni de allá © A J Bermudez, 2020
Return © Neil Lawrence, 2020
Rewilding © Jackie Taylor, 2020
Roots © Patience Mackarness, 2020
Sir Thomas Wyatt's Cat © Elinor Brooks, 2020
Sirius © Jane Aldous, 2020
Sketchbook © Jane McLaughlin, 2020
Slow Burn © Julian Bishop, 2020
The Saddest Birdes a Season Find to Singe © Kelly Davis, 2020
Turner's World of Twirls © Margaret Crompton, 2020
Twelve Point Plan © Pippa Gladhill, 2020
When Naked Plants Renew © Keely O'Shaughnessy, 2020

TYMES GOE BY TURNES

Contents

Introduction
Cherry Potts

Before I ran Arachne Press, I did many things, including, for a while, a job I hated. While in that job, I had as my screensaver/lock/background the words

Tymes Goe By Turnes, and Chaunces Chang by Course

I felt better every time I saw them.

Looking back, it's obvious I should have left the job, rather than comfort myself with the fact that something else would cause a change.

The lines are from Robert Southwell (c.1561 – 21 February 1595), who had plenty to be worried about. Look him up if you want to feel better about your current situation by comparison. If that's not the sort of comfort that moves you, (me neither) read the poem, which follows at the end of this introduction; it'll work better, promise.

With the arrival of Covid-19 and lockdown, I decided I could worry myself to death, or take a leaf from Southall's tree and look beyond to better times that might, *if* we do something about it, reappear. I am a planner by nature, so I planned the bits I could, and waited to see what chances changed by which courses. At the time of writing we think this year's Solstice Shorts Festival will have to be online, but there *will* be a festival, and there *is* a book; and Southall's poem provided an excellent Covid-haunted time theme for the festival and the book.

We asked for stories and poems that responded or reacted or were inspired by the poem or some concept in it.

We wanted change, finding balance, release… and we got them.

Tymes Goe By Turnes by Robert Southall

The lopped tree in tyme may grow agayne;
Most naked plants renew both frute and floure;
The soriest wight may find release of payne,
The dryest soyle suck in some moystning shoure;
Tymes go by turnes and chaunces chang by course,
From foule to fayre, from better happ to worse.

The sea of Fortune doth not ever floe,
She drawes her favours to the lowest ebb;
Her tyde hath equall tymes to come and goe,
Her loom doth weave the fine and coarsest webb;
No joy so great but runneth to an ende,
No happ so harde but may in fine amende.

Not allwayes fall of leafe nor ever spring,
No endless night yet not eternall daye;
The saddest birdes a season find to singe,
The roughest storme a calm may soone alaye;
Thus with succeding turnes God tempereth all,
That man may hope to rise yet feare to fall.

A chaunce may wynne that by mischance was lost;
The nett that houldes no greate, takes little fish;
In some thinges all, in all thinges none are croste,
Fewe all thcy neede, but none have all they wishe;
Unmedled joyes here no man befall,
Who least hath some, who most hath never all.

The lopped tree
    in tyme may grow agayne;

Most naked plants renew
    both frute and floure;

The soriest wight
    may find release of payne,

The dryest soyle suck in
    some moystning shoure;

Tymes go by turnes and
    chaunces chang by course,

From foule to fayre,
    from better happ to worse.

A Felled Tree
Brooke Stanicki

The morning after he left, she was empty dirt, a space where a person used to be. He had lopped off pieces of her from the minute that he knew she had fallen in love. Like a felled tree, he didn't have use for her leaves, the frontiers of her mind growing into empty space in her once boundless sky. No need for new frontiers, he wanted utility from his wife.

She would never forget the first time his threats turned into wounds. the time when he had too much to drink and burned bits of her personality to keep his ego warm. No need for her to grow, he was a blanket over her. He kept her warm and safe and airless.

How could she breathe again, without his strict instructions on how to breathe and when?

How could she learn to live when most of her years had been lived on her behalf? He said that only he could possibly love her, only he could love her naked; so, of course, she didn't love herself.

She hated mirrors almost as much as she hated the plants in her window box, they got to grow in beautiful colours. Each season, they got to die, and renew, and start over.

She was constrained to live in the bounds of black and white because both she and her dreams needed to be paused for his ambitions.

In return, she got the fruit of his labour and a side of his bed and every poisonous drop of his private hatred and public compliments.

A generous husband, he would say.

He would never let her speak or grow or flower; *a generous husband,* he would say, *would never let her make the mistake of living.*

The funny thing was that she agreed. Who was she to know what exactly was best for her? Her, the sorest charity case that he saw, and so generously, so selflessly, took. The lucky, chosen, blessed wight that got his attention, that got his last name.

Her family was shocked, they had thought that she would never find someone to love her. And to them, he looked like love, because how could they know what was happening behind closed doors? How could they know that her soul was begging for release, when her words never said such a thing?

She needed him to breathe, remember?

She lost all her friends when he found her. He didn't like her friends. They saw early pain in her eyes. They smelled his wolf breath. But they couldn't know for sure what he was.

The way he looked at her – it could have been love. Or possession. Or hatred. Or just the very driest form of love. Who were they to know?

When he left, and she was reduced to soil, how was she supposed to think about a better future? He had the power to suck her dreams right out of her. This had been her dream, to live in a nice house with a nice husband. He was a nice husband. Nice husbands, of course, usually have some less-than-nice things they do. Like smoke cigarettes or forget the trash or hit wives. Soon, she stopped dreaming.

Tears moistened her cheeks. She didn't look thirty-two. She only looked thirty-two when she wore makeup or took a shower – water washed some years away, he added a few, by force. Because all those terrible, awful times that his dinner wasn't perfect, he needed to teach her a lesson.

Why would she decide to go? She wouldn't. She couldn't. She needed him to breathe.

Of course, he could go out with the guys. by which he meant, go out with other women. A good player of the game, he knew how to make his turns count. She knew he was going out more. Maybe, just maybe, she knew – maybe the smell of perfume was just from a coworker. The chances were high that he was just wearing a new cologne, right? And he spilled it and didn't want to change – nor change out of lipstick-stained shirts – but she didn't say anything. She washed them because that was her job, and by doing her job correctly, she thought that she could keep him from leaving. That was wrong, of course, he left.

After making her reliant on him, after cutting all her leaves, after covering her from sunlight to make sure she wouldn't grow, he left, for someone new – someone with life for his foul talons to carve into, someone with brilliance that needed to be extinguished.

And she was left to figure out what life was like without him. She couldn't breathe. *How is this fair,* she thought, *that he can breathe, and I cannot?*

She had thought that it was luck, some incredible hap, that they had met. She had been so thankful that he taught her to live. But how could he have taught her to live, when her growth was against his rules? She had been convinced that a world without him would be worse. But now, left with a rich network of roots, she realised that her life with him had been barren.

And yes, she was breathing, free from his instruction.

She took off his blanket, and found that although the world was cold, it was very, very bright.

When Naked Plants Renew
Keely O'Shaughnessy

On the evening our neighbours bring their new baby girl home, I'm looking out at the street and watch them arrive. The orchids that line our windowsill tremble as their car pulls up.

'Are they back?' Jen calls from the kitchen.

'Nothing yet.'

They shut off the headlights and then the guy, I think his name is Liam, helps his wife from the passenger's side. They both stop and coo at the child, and viewed through the curtain's net, the edges of this new family tableau are softened into watercolour.

My voice sounds small and strange in the lie and I wonder if Jen might come out anyway. Seeing them there she would note their stretched, immovable smiles and say something like, *Isn't that great for them?* or *What a cutie, eh?* and, despite her shrugging, I'd feel the knot in her belly tightening just as it does in mine.

We've tried for years, waiting for the magic to happen: for Jen's stomach to swell and fill up those hairline cracks that can't be plugged or sealed by anything else. We've followed all the advice and seen handfuls of specialists. It takes time is my favourite. Like that's all that's required.

For a while, after they've gone inside, I stay by the window. First, I pick at the mesh of the curtain and then at one of the orchid's wide, fleshy leaves. At the end of a thick stem is a cluster of three glossy, green buds. Orchids grow painfully slowly. This one, The Circle of Life, if it blooms, will send out broad, vivid-red petals with a central flute that looks something like a vulva. This is the lip or labellum. I know this because Jen knows this. She knows that the throat of a Moth Orchid looks like the all-seeing eye of a leopard's pelt and that an orchid can so easily stop or fail to grow – too much light and they scorch, too much water and their compost becomes inhospitable.

Tonight, Jen is making Tuscan chicken, which we'll eat while she talks about the time we toured the Palazzo Pitti. And then later, after finishing a bottle of Tignanello, she'll tell me how Florence is a beautiful girl's name.

I listen as Jen pours out the wine. She slurps from hers and tops it up. The house is too quiet, so I switch on the TV and return to my post at the window.

The streetlights flicker on and the neighbour's front door opens again. This time, just Liam emerges with the buggy. He paces up the street undulating the buggy as he walks. He does a loop of the cul-de-sac before doubling back and stopping just beyond the path that separates our properties. He checks his phone. Screen glare illuminates his face. I could take the baby. Slip out and slip back while he's busy scrolling Twitter. Liam's eyes are heavy, already sleep-deprived, he'd barely notice. The baby's formative memory hasn't yet developed. She hasn't had a chance to imprint. She'd come to know only my voice, my cadence, my timbre. The fantasy evaporates as Liam bumps the buggy up the front step before they both disappear inside.

When Jen comes in, she hands me my glass and gestures towards next-door's car.

'I think we just missed them,' I say.

'I got a present. A bunny-toy-rattle-thing.' A neatly wrapped present, adorned with a teddy bear shaped tag, sits on the stairs.

'They need time to adjust, Jenny. They don't need us lurking around.' I put my arm around her, but she's already inspecting the orchids for new growth.

After pollination, it takes some orchids months to flower. Jen knows this; I know this. Yet, for a moment, I think I see the bud on The Circle of Life move. I say something to Jen about the wine, a crass but witty line about roofies. She doesn't reply and squeezes the orchid plant food dropper that's stuck upright in its pot. And then, at time-lapse speed, the dome of petals pulsates and grows.

The growth is exponential. Within a minute, it has doubled in size. And then tripled. I check to see Jen is seeing what I am. She interlaces her hand in mine and squats low to the ground. We breathe together. Slow breaths to start with, growing until we are panting.

I think of the fertility talisman that is kept locked in the drawer of Jen's nightstand: a souvenir from Kenya. Carved from walnut, its engorged breasts are etched with spirals. If I found it now, I'm sure its eyes would be glowing, feeding on something from deep within us. In my head, the wooden talisman takes on a cartoonish quality, the green of the glow far too fluorescent to be real. Yet, there's a part of me that accepts this primal event for what it is – uniquely biological.

It's strange, but I know what's happening, like looking at the sun with your eyes closed – there's a warmth, an intensity, the sense of something more. Beneath the plant's dorsal sepal, an embryo is forming. The stem dips and bows under the pressure of this new weight. A mass of pollen and sinew, the bud has ballooned to the size of a large watermelon. The flower's column is now so stretched the outline of a tiny foot is visible. Its shape is embossed on the petals for a second before it dissipates.

I reach for Jen and haul her up from the carpet.

'This is happening,' I say.

My voice is shaky and her breathing is ragged. From behind us, an advert for life insurance is on the TV. Its jingle some tinny elevator music.

'The Tuscan chicken,' Jen says, 'It's burning.'

'I know,' I say.

Placing our hands around the bloom, the tap-tap, tap-tap of a heartbeat is unmistakable.

Bringing in the Fruit
Claire Booker

Our little tree is the height of a man –
scuffed with age, chain-mailed in spit-grey lichen.

We arrive when it's breaking into leaf.
It may be apple or pear; plum or

even peach. It may be barren. So we wait.
For bees, for sunlight.

Scanty blossoms begin to unboll, white as cotton.
Sometimes a dove paddles in its branches,

fills them with cooing. The little tree drags its anchor
through dry and chalky soil. All we can do

is keep hosing through the rainless weeks. Tiny plum
embryos, green and hard, take up position

and start to swell. They're like children
to us now – the loss of even one puts a scab on the day.

Some fall to knots of orange-rimmed slugs.
Some shrivel, some thrive.

A blackbird sprints towards the boom
of purple with a lascivious eye.

Rewilding
Jackie Taylor

She always used to join in with the chatter and banter because there was really no choice, not in normal, everyday life. But she'd always tended towards the quiet.

During the first phase of the panic, there were online meetings, voices on voices, staggered stops and pile-ups of words and stutters and silences. No-one noticed that she was the one who muted first, who clicked on a thumbs-up instead of speaking, who mimed her way through. And then the meetings fizzled out anyway, as the tech started to falter and networks were commandeered for other purposes. Connections and nodes crackled and died. It was inevitable. It heralded the second phase of world-wide panic, when -

Dog-rose became eglantine, hawthorn became may, as weeks passed and the orders to stay at home came to her by megaphone from the sky. As months passed, her reversions continued. Honeysuckle became woodbine, aquilegia became columbine, and her language circled back on itself, rewinding, rewilding, her tongue becoming whole and wholesome again. The old words were easier on the tongue and gentler on the belly. She could stomach them and keep them down.

She stayed at home. She noticed the ragged robin and cuckoo flower. She began to feel the length of the day-span instead of measuring it. There was time to harvest wild garlic, elderflower, wild strawberry, elderberry.

Sparrows colonised the wheel arches of the car that went nowhere. She'd always left windings of hair from her comb, out by the door for new nestings, but she cut out the middleman and went direct, offering her shoulder for jackdaws and others to sit on and pull loose threads from her jumper, or take what they needed straight from her head. And if she needed to speak to a magpie or crow, why would she use her own words? It was all so obvious. It was only natural.

She worried sometimes that she might lose words altogether, and if that happened, how would thinking be done? But it was worth the risk, and she liked her new ways.

After the third wave, the threat subsided. She'd lost the way of counting by months, but knew that four longest nights had passed. It was the planes coming back that told her it was over. She wept at the sky and the fresh vapour trails that bisected and straight-lined the blue.

She started to hear cars again, out in the distance, when the wind blew from that way. Would they come to her? She wasn't ready. There had never been much traffic down the lane, her lane, only the lost, but still, the thought of people being able to drive past her cottage at any odd time, and suppose they stopped and knocked, people in cars, and asked for directions? What would she… what would she… would she be able to … if somebody asked, what would she say? People would ask, because anyone driving down her lane was going to be lost and needing directions to the nearest big place.

The first car was not lost people, but a van with the postman. A different one, it had been a long time, and he wasn't to know.

He had thin, shiny papers about pizza deliveries and UPVC windows, all newly reopened for her business. He knocked on her door out of politeness to let her know that normal was back. His eyes were black with sunglasses. She had to concentrate hard to decipher his words. She smiled at him and nodded, then shut the door, awkward and fumbling with shaking hands and sick to the pit of her stomach.

When she walked down the lane that evening, there was a dead baby rabbit. Run over by the postman, small blood on the lane-way, eyes widely open. She left it for jackdaws. Early next morning, she cut branches of blackthorn and laid them out across the lane. She didn't need much, the way was so narrow, more like a tunnel, and dark with tree-shadows.

Blackthorn like needles for stitching of leather. The postman's tyre flattened. He came on foot, knocked at her door, and she couldn't see his eyes again because of the blackness but she knew he was angry because of his loudness, even though she couldn't fasten onto his speakings. She opened her mouth to make words back to him, but the words didn't come and she was left standing in her doorway with her mouth wide, wide open but silent, as the postman walked away, back down the lane and –

It took time for her to close her mouth shut, even after he'd gone. She just wasn't able. She wondered then whether she should make some effort. Had her life slipped too far off its fulcrum to be rebalanced? Was it too late to unlock and re-engage her voice? But she felt no need to re-join the cumulative noise of the world, or to add to it in any way. Even if she could. There was no going back, and she wondered how many, like her, had found new, better ways.

Sometimes she still opens her mouth, just to see what will happen but she can't – she just can't – push the words out. Not even the old words, the ones that are easier on the tongue and gentler on the belly, the old words she can swallow and keep down in her body.

a memory forgotten
Sean Carney

life feeds life;
peonies emerge
from dirty bulbs
who feasted on

petals of last year's peony

when you appreciate
the pinks and whites
scattered across the lawn
do you stop to ask the soil

When did you forget
you were a flower?

In Dark
Karen Ankers

In dark we are seed, we are
 Colour-mould leaf-scent, raw
warp and weft – in dark
the light grows that bursts from first sun.

No boundaries in dark,
no limits,
 no need –
dandelion secrets
hoarded like gold, swell
promises: listen: lay
ear to earth, press
lip to soil;

hear seeds dream of summer –
let the darkness
 be.

Turner's World of Twirls
Margaret Crompton

Tina pirouettes dizzily round the floor, collides with Wayne, and collapses at my feet. 'So sorry, Miss Bobby.'

'No problem. Only a rehearsal. But tomorrow –'

'I'll be perfect. Promise. Can I have another turn?'

'Keep to the outside of the circle. You're the tip of the second hand. Flicky twirls leading us to –'

'Midday. I know.'

Midday. December 21st. After they've spun themselves giddy, and relieved relations have whirled them away home for the last time, I'll take down the signboard. Farewell, TURNER'S WORLD OF TWIRLS.

They'll lie, 'Wish you weren't going, Miss. We'll miss you.'

I'll lie in return, 'I'll miss you, too.' Because I won't. Because I never do. In any case, they'll be seeing me again, Tina and Wayne. Although they won't know it's me.

Tomorrow is my last appearance as Roberta Turner. Miss Bobby. *Esteemed exponent of Ballet, Tap and Musical Theatre.* When I began, ten years ago, I enjoyed it. I always do relish the new challenge. Congratulate myself on My Ideal Deal. Not one of those stupid *Anything you like for a hundred years in exchange for your immortal soul* contracts, or *Eternal Life* (forgetting to stipulate Age Range 17-45), or even that idiotic *Eternal Youth*, landing themselves in nappies and sucking dummies for eternity. Dumb or what!

I always relish this moment, when my next future's about to turn up. My time for looking back. Beginning in the so-called 'Middle Ages'. Middle of what? There I am, isolated in

25

that chilly cell, ignoring the summons to Sext. (Do they still giggle at that? Not for long, if Novice Director's taking a turn round the cloister). Midday. Meditating on death on an empty stomach. Bored out of my skull. Without thinking, I say out loud, 'What wouldn't I give for a change?'(in Latin, naturally). Totally forgetting it's Solstice. Bad timing? Good? Who knows?

What *did* I give? Certainly not my soul, or freedom, or life. The only fee is the Decadal Review. No small print. I keep rules, tick boxes. Just the one niggle. I preferred reporting in person. I confess to relief when austerity eradicated lightning flashes and fiery whirlwinds. But I valued personal contact. Human to – Non-human. A little word of encouragement goes a long way, especially in those doldrum decades when the sea of fortune hasn't flowed too fortunately. I'd welcome being welcomed into the next Change, whatever it turns out to be. It can be lonely, leaving one life and starting the next, with no one to miss me. Or welcome me. Yes, everything changes. But ticking boxes is, dare I whisper, one change too far. There's no soul in a tedious tick like an upside-down tenterhook. Not that I'm on tenterhooks about this report, rounding off another successful decade.

What Changes did I negotiate?

1. *Gender* (turn and turn about)
2. *Age* (post-nappy/dummy)
3. *Location* (remain within area formerly occupied by Abbey: furnishings, equipment, etc. replaced, as appropriate)
4. *Occupation* (linked with surname). Leads to intriguing encounters when we come across one another. Fellow dramatist John Webster, I remember, weaving words into webs of hopeful rises and fearful falls. As Master Cyril Tourneur, I penned some powerful plays myself, but who's heard of me now? Hard to garner a reputation when you're always going and coming.

Like Webster the weaver, I can always turn a neat phrase.

Enjoyed my poetic decade as Ursula T. Urn. Published *The Speaking Sundial.* Following Miss Urn's mysterious disappearance before she could unleash her proposed sequel, Cousin Josiah lost no time in establishing his horological workshop and showroom, TIME GOES BY, in her elegant villa. That century was good for me, one Change leading smoothly onward. When Josiah moved his business into larger premises, Mrs Netty Trundle, a middle-aged widow, opened the first tourist bureau in the borough. The tours she organised were so successful that, after ten lucrative years, she herself took to globe-trotting.

For centuries, I regretted that I'd never even seen a tournament, blaming my father for donating me to the Abbey when I'd been too young for those state-of-the-art sporting sensations. Father was Robert le Turnor, whose hubs kept the Abbey cartwheels turning, and supported my admission to the novitiate. But what goes around comes around and after a few centuries, Sir Ralph Tournour's inherited fortune funded TOURNAMENTS ARE US. The former Abbey gardens converted into impressive lists with a comfortable pavilion (all modern conveniences) and signed souvenir pennants. Sir Ralph turned a triumphant profit from hiring Medieval costumes, entrance fees, and jousting classes.

Less successful was a decade during some Civil War or another, although Lady Honour earned admiration for her tender touch with a tourniquet. Since she had inconsiderately supported the losing side, the Abbey was partly demolished and wholly plundered. Her retirement to a retreat for landless ladies coincided with the return of her son, the talented turncoat Lord Janus, who reversed the family misfortunes.

One of my favourites was Charming Charlie with his Abbey Gardens Carousel. Turned out of town one chilly winter's day, his only profits were in fun. Florence, Charlie's divorced wife, claimed the site for maintenance and established a children's playground with whirligigs and fortune-floating candy-floss. Charlie's brother, comedian Laughing Lonnie, lost the lot with his too-near-the-bone satirical Comic Turns. But long-lost Auntie Vera from Vegas turned up trumps with her money-spinning Casino. I loved being Auntie V. in her laced and lacy basque.

And so it goes. While I've been revolving many memories, I've tenterhooked all the boxes. The new signboard's ready.

TIRED TOES TWINKLE
AT
MISTER TOBIAS TURNER'S
ACADEMY
OF
OLDE TYME
TERPSICHOREAN
WALTZES & WHIRLS

Wayne and Tina will be back, to watch their grandparents rotating in their own end-of-year performances.

I wonder, sometimes, what it would be like to stop. Stop twirling, whirling, Turning. My Ideal Deal somehow omitted to mention Ending. After Tobias, it will be time to welcome Dame Portia Turner, LLB, Consultant in Contract Law.

Return
Neil Lawrence

Minus wakes. Sits up, pulls at the back of his neck but all pain has gone. Turns his head, sees his left arm regrown into the suit. The hand pink as a new-born.

Here... how?

Not sure.

Teeth clench. Nothing. No explanation comes.

But he *is* Minus. He knows *that*.

And this field. This field. It was dead, shrivelled up. Barren. Not so now.

He rises from his bed, from fractured wood... what has happened?

He walks the field, something ritualistic in his low, hunkered gait.

Something had burst up from the blistered ground. Clumps of – of newness.

White fringes the yellow face, like a lion's mane.

Flowers? Are they...? Yet the ground still carries the familiar stench.

He releases the breath he has been holding, surprised there is no urge to vomit.

He tugs at the glove protecting his right hand; it gives way with a squeak, a pop. Skin on the back of his hand the colour of stone. Angry webbing between his fingers, scaly and raw, not yet healed. Yet the wind that plays between his fingers is mercifully cool.

It takes a long time, but he allows himself to touch – to

stroke – one of the large green buds of a plant not yet in leaf. There is relief; no pain. His skin does not break or seep or swell. The feeling beneath his fingertips... It has been *such* a long time... He remembers the first soft bristling of hair above his lips... fourteen, fifteen? He remembers the downiness, the feel beneath his fingers...

'Lamb's Ears.'

From nothing the name comes. It comes in the voice of his father. His father who must have given those words to him, given him that name.

Minus sighs. He stands, ready for the past.

The memory is bright. He can smell... the kitchen, his father – his sweat. Still healthy then, his smell. Schools had been closed by then. For a year? Everyone ordered inside by then, but the windows? He is not sure.

'When the earth cools, we can plant.' His father's voice, so cool, so gentle. But perhaps that is his memory. There are things of which he *is* certain. He remembers the seeds. He remembers how bored he was. He remembers his father starting to cough. How he'd hoped, hopelessly that it wasn't, that it couldn't be...

Minus reaches the streambed, its channel worn deep into the earth. He remembers Bliss following the stream downhill, that *last* summer.

Bliss, running after the water as though she could escape with it, as though she could disappear with it. As if she could *go*...

He looks down, shocked to see a return.

An infinitesimal vein of fluid gleams within the bed. *It came back,* he thinks.

Minus lies down, opens the mesh flap that hides his face, and dips his tongue into the trickle. He shivers, runs the flat of his tongue across the stream bed. Moist grit and soft earth.

He stays there until the root of his tongue aches. Then he stands, groaning, groping for the catch at the back of his helmet.

When, finally, it gives, he hears a tearing sound. It sheers through his skull. The top of his head smarts. He reaches up, his fingers probing at the crown, finding wetness. Hair missing. The blood it brings to the surface, the blood on his palm is red.

Red blood.

Healthy blood.

This is not pain, he thinks. *This is celebration.*

This is… revelation?

Minus walks to the farmhouse, a concrete husk; windows uselessly, pointlessly boarded – the door is gone. He passes the makeshift shelter in the lounge, constructed with Bliss in those last desperate months. Modified sheep wool. Stuffed sheets. An attempt at insulation. They lay listening in the dark, for sounds – the tell-tale sounds of deterioration.

Minus remembers, hard and sudden, that final night. The sounds. The smell. Father's ungovernable sores. Everything ungovernable.

He climbs the pock-marked stairs. Enters a bedroom. His parents' bedroom. A desiccated wardrobe belches out grit and stone. Inside it, a green nightgown, clinging to a rusty hanger by thin straps. A tan lab coat. The initials on the chest faded.

Mother's or Father's? He can't tell.

He lies down on the bed.

Ragged splinters from somewhere puncture the skin of his neck. He doesn't care.

Mother... Mum.

He thinks of her at the end. Coughing. Lying on her side. The bucket. Parts of her in the bucket.

She said something – Renew? Return? He'd not been listening, not realising he'd not hear her voice again.

From downstairs now, a sound. A sneeze. A cough? A bark? It brings Minus back.

He goes down to the kitchen. Whimpering. There is whimpering, growing louder.

From the sink. The stained, brown sink.

In there is a *Darrem* dog. Gene spliced. *Dankin* bred. A Darrem dog, its nose against the rusting plug hole. Bites pit the fur, ribs visible, but the coat is still thick, a mustardy yellow, the eyes are bright. Tubular tongue probes the basin. Minus rubs a palm against the flat of the dog's head. Pencil-shaped tail bobs. Minus scoops her out. The Dankin hums, contented.

Outside, Minus takes the dog to the streambed. Her tongue sweeps the earth. Her tail bobs. She looks up, chin well gritted, yips.

Minus waits a moment. Then another. Then he smiles, climbs down into the streambed with the dog.

They follow its path together, past the field where he woke. They are going. Minus knows they are going to the wood. The wood that was once an escape from the heat. That awful, mutated heat. That hideous pressure rippling across the fields, between the trees, through everything.

Through everyone.

Back inside after that. Everyone forced back inside. And how long had Mother and Father lasted afterwards? Days? Hours? It hadn't mattered. Time became pointless. Useless. Unknowable.

But Mother... Not for her...

'All will return,' Minus tells the Dankin.

Just as Mother had told him… he is almost sure that's what she said.

The stream bed dips, the trickle deepens. He glimpses shoots of new grass here and there.

And another smell, one he recognises.

'Lavender.'

His father's voice again.

Minus whistles. The Dankin is distracted – a fly, of all things, the first Minus remembers seeing since –

For a long time he stands. Then he lifts his hand to the seal of his suit. He tugs.

But the zip will not move.

He pleads. With whom, he doesn't know.

The Dankin leaps up. Her eyes purple, characteristic, for her breed, of worry.

At last, something gives. Minus cries out. A fingernail, his fingernail, long and yellow, rends the weakened lining. He tears. Fabric falls in strips like old wallpaper.

Laughter, hoarse and high.

The light is dimming, but this is not a sign of trouble. There is peace in this darkness.

The colours of the heavens are like the song his sister sang – her voice, high and out of tune. It made Minus laugh. Only Bliss could make him laugh like that.

'The sky returns from blister red
To clean and hope and blue instead.'

But as the house grew colder, Bliss's voice stopped being funny.

And the strawberries, too, had stopped smelling happy. Minus had wept. Wept and wept, clutching his empty belly as she sang the same words over and over.

Minus cries. He has reached the bottom of the hill, where Bliss used to come. Where she used to follow the stream. He wipes his eyes. The once proud wood, not gone. Not completely.

One…two…three… *ten* short, skinny trunks.

The bark is clean, untinged by the orange blight that broke so many in the before time.

The striplings stand proud, raw recruits.

Past them, the stream feeds a small pond.

Minus cannot stop. He scoops water, throws it over his chest. Rubs it into his skin.

Behind him, footsteps approach.

He leans forward, repeats the blessing of water.

All will return.

The sound of breathing from behind him.

Eyes closed now. Water slaps his face.

Then a gasp.

In this place of so much silence he hears lips part.

A high, thin voice.

The sky returns…

Minus leans back and arms are ready, waiting to wrap around him.

He feels her hold him, and take a deep breath, and he rises with her breath.

Her song goes through his body. Just as in the before.

Her voice is frail, but its playfulness has returned.

…To clean and hope and blue instead.

The sea of Fortune
doth not ever floe,

She drawes her favours
to the lowest ebb:

Her tyde hath equall tymes
to come and goe,

Her loom doth weave the fine
and coarsest webb:

No joy so great
but runneth to an ende,

No happ so harde
but may in fine amende.

For Ellen
S B Merrow

That far off summer of sixty-one,
suntanned mad on Mayo Beach—

our salty bodies twin buoys
above the rippled floor of the bay

whose wavy fathoms lifted us,
girls of seven—who even then

knew something of frailty—your
sunny tendrils of mermaid hair

weightless as song—we are dolphins,
arms stretched into snouts, the rest

a muscle's afterthought—legs clamped
together as fins, we dive

along the shore, probing the endless
ocean.

This solstice,

a sharp-beaked falcon tops the elm—
unworried about future or past,

he hails the darkness with *kek, kek*
accompaniment, cocks an eye to meet

our gaze, turning yellow breast
into the glow above the houses—while

our grownup hands, featherless and finless,
bundle cold greens—juniper and yew,

spruce, magnolia—into looping garlands,
the fires around us still burning.

In the Rocks
Lynn White

It was a small gap
in the rocks
dry and bare
for a time
in waiting,
waiting
for the tide
to turn
and the sea
to wash through
to leave it
not quite dry;

a trickle
of salt water
left behind,
salt tears
running down a face,
pooling below
full of life
full of creatures
brought back to life.
Tears can sometimes do that
temporarily.

Ni de aquí, ni de allá
A J Bermudez

The water is warmer than she remembers
frothing with a Castile soap sheen of detritus.
Beside her, the girl chalks a moon-shaped indent in the hull of
the raft with her nail,
        opalescent on dark skin
                freckled with salt.
'Where will we say we are from?' the girl asks.
'Ni de aquí, ni de allá.'
'And where are we going?'
In the distance, a clutter of
        buildings,
                ships,
                        rafts
        sprout from the hazy arc of the earth.
She considers the sky, aching blue, every colour at once,
        imagines it shedding like a snake,
                flecks of clouds like skin on the surface of the sea.
'The world is not a ball but a mountain.'
'But where are we *going?*'
In her eyes are not water but forests,
        every tree that will one day be
                a book,
                        an atlas,
                                a dwelling.

Beach Clean
Ness Owen

This year we only
find left footed shoes.
We wonder where all
the right ones have
gone and how we'd
walk without them.
The slower we move
the more we discover
sifting through the
plastic ruins, freeing
bladder wrack from
the choke of net.
We find a piece shaped
just like Bridget's cross
underneath some quartz
stones. *A sign*, you say.
Following the trail of
shore-crab moults, we
reach washed-up goat
willow, roots already
darkening. One branch
shows life in leaves and
catkin. A gentle tap
releases the seeds and
carries them up-shore.

Snowflakes hoping for
ground. The sea-wind
brushes the sky with
grey. They'd promised
rain and there's comfort
in the uncertainty of the
sky, the fall of thunder-
drops and the sweet
smell of summer's rain.

Deep Blue Sea
Linda McMullen

The resort offers a limited array of beverages with paper umbrellas in exchange for mild-to-moderate attention during their mandatory 3:45 timeshare presentation. I select a sweating azure glass after the commission-fed minions conclude their 'low-pressure' pitch: *It's five o'clock somewhere… right now!*

Maddie brushes Rainbow Dash's muzzle against my unshaved calves for the twelfth time. I fantasise about grinding the Pegasus wannabe into glitter beneath my heel. 'Can we go swimming NOW, Mommy?'

'Before you go,' interjects a blond salesminion, whose only possible name is Chad, 'I'd love to show you a one-bedroom-plus loft, just available –'

'Sorry,' I reply, as Maddie repeats her demand with increasing speed, ferocity, and volume, 'I'd better get someone out of here.'

'The unit has its own pool,' Chad begins, causing Maddie to pause. My paper umbrella dissolves in a swirl of curaçao mid-sip, and I set my beverage down.

'Look. I won this getaway weekend in a prize draw at Chili's. Maddie and I ate there after my now ex-husband embezzled enough to fully escape our daughter's teen years in a medium-security facility, but not enough to secure a lavish exile in Argentina. So, I'm not really in a position to commit right now.'

Chad's one-week Gordon Gekko-lite training somehow failed to cover this particular eventuality.

'MOMMY CAN WE –'

'YES, Maddie.'

Wake, breakfast, cartoons, pool. Bathroom break, pool. Snack, pool, bathroom break, pool, five minutes later back to the bathroom, pool. Lunch. Screams that I am UNFAIR and she is BORED and everything is HORRIBLE because I insist on walking up the miniscule Main Street for an hour before returning to the POOL (Maddie extorted four new ponies in exchange for a restrained fracas). Truthfully, I got as far as the clinic walkway, seven years ago. The protestors had taken the day off: no gauntlet of signs blazed before me. They might have stoked my courage. Instead: hasty cubic zirconia, courthouse smoke-break, matchbox sublet, goodbye to making partner.

POOL. Bathroom. POOL. Snack. Thirty minutes of my enduring amazement that she doesn't go hoarse. High needs, special needs, emotionally needy in the face of an absent father, spin the Wheel of Bottomless Requirement. Also: Maddie doesn't swim. Won't. Can't? I exist only to bear her at mermaid height through her aquamarine realm.

POOL.

After her: Hugh's newfound careerism. He hissed, 'Shit!' tripping over Maddie's plastic detritus as he departed from, and returned to, our dark apartment. And also when the red-and-blue lights traced the popcorn of our bedroom ceiling.

POOL.

Now, four tween boys risk cracked skulls by cannonballing into the four-foot depths. Maddie shrieks as the splashes sting her eyes, then cries when I suggest another activity.

'What if we try the beach for a few minutes?' I ask.

Another torrent hits her face; she coughs, sputters, nods.

The ponies, apparently, change color in water. Maddie consents to drown/revive them independently while I recline on a towel and order a new Deep Blue Sea Martini, *sans parapluie.* Maddie wades out, out into the blue, to submerge her ponies, herself. The drink is eight-tenths pineapple juice. A small stream of bubbles liberates itself from her lips… at a plausible distance.

I mull the possible headlines: *Beachside tragedy. Too late. But not her fault.*

Not her fault.

I set the drink down, execute a few quick strokes, pull Maddie out, beat her only a little too hard on the back. She smiles wanly at me as the ponies drift back to shore.

Piano Lessons
Claire Booker

She smelt of stale biscuits; had fingers the colour of custard.
We sat tandem on the piano stool, while gap-toothed children stared
from the wall, clutching certificates. It was only a matter of time,
she promised. Some children took to it quickly. Some not.

Sharps and flats basked like crocodiles in the shallows; pulled me
kicking under the water. Follow the beat, she intoned,
as the metronome clicked its tongue – forced me to sprint,
when all I could do was limp. We started on the *Bluebell Waltz*

in May – a slippery little tune, with killer teeth. I howled inside
at each wrong note, as if I'd killed a bird. We hammered away at it
through June, until she licked her pencil and re-christened
the piece *Rose Waltz*, as though the seasons could hide my shame.

Flowers kept blooming across the score. *Mistletoe Waltz* arrived
for Christmas, when she gave me *A Little Book of Gardening* in tissue
paper. Think of the pedal as an extra hand. But there wasn't room
in my head for three hands. And snowdrops began to break out.

The sheet music, with its many scrawls, stood open in readiness.
She paused, but didn't pick up the pencil. Have you thought
of telling your mother you'd like to stop? We looked at each other
in wonder. I could never have thought of that.

Not allwayes fall of leafe
                    nor ever spring,
No endless night
                    yet not eternall daye;

The saddest birdes
                    a season find to singe,

The roughest storme
                    a calm may soone alaye;

Thus with succeding turnes
                    God tempereth all,

That man may hope to rise
                    yet feare to fall.

Slow Burn
Julian Bishop

Long-life bulbs take an age to warm,
their filaments flickering
like street-lights at the turn of day.

Under the pale sodium glow of January
crops of snowdrops shiver into growth,
their moth-wing petals only unfurling

in cool February sun. The brighter light
ignites aconites, warms a crocus,
tickles saffron stamens into flames,

sets a torch to celandines. March adds
a glowing crown to towering Imperials,
radiance to the wide-eyed narcissi

while tulips save their match-tip flames
for April. A low gas glow of bluebells
rises from leafy debris in May,

until spring is as distant as winter.
If we wait long enough, tropical cannas
will rip wildfire through the borders.

Cronos
Laila Sumpton

my father said Saturn
was an old castle wall
half at the point of falling
half at the point of growing
the moment you linger
between mallet or trowel
and the unbuilt turret
shivers in your mind

Father Time paces
humming a tune half known
as you tease out the threads
from a hem unfurling
as the evening dances
you round
and here's the one thing
that never changes

the prayer at the sky
right before dusking
for you to be swallowed
and swathed in that exact
and changing shade
because there are stars
just waiting

The Saddest Birdes a Season Find to Singe
Kelly Davis

This spring
we heard them all –
not just strident gulls
but blackbirds, meadow pipits, larks,
sparrows, starlings, cuckoos, doves.

As traffic faded
birds grabbed the microphone –
and they were full of the joys.
They laughed and shouted,
strutting like Jagger.

Behind our locked doors,
we bit our nails,
washed our hands,
watched news reports,
waiting for our feathers to grow.

Twelve Point Plan
Pippa Gladhill

One.
First of all, don't look back.

Two.
Look out of the window instead. Holy crap. It's now summer. How did that happen? Well, duh, summer comes along after spring. It happens each year, regardless. And, yes, see, plums are falling from the plum tree. They could be made into jam. Good plan. Allow your enthusiasm room. Even though you don't like jam. When it's done, line up the seven jars on the shelf. Then, re arrange them into descending size order, largest to the left, smallest to the right, because, why not. Also, make plum crumble. Freeze it, in easy to use, single, portions.

Three.
Advise the cat it's not meal time yet. Then maybe look around for what's been forgotten. Clock the *Lonely Planet Guide to Italy* on the kitchen table where it's been for many months. It's a library book. Check online when it was due back. Whoa, the overdue fine will be massive, and growing bigger by the minute. Ponder a moment. Feel pretty sure libraries have declared an overdue book amnesty. At this point, do nothing for a while. Instead, stroke the cat, and pick up the book. Let it fall open onto page … 188, and read that *Cremona is a small town in the middle of the Po plain renowned for its violins.* Really? Note this interesting fact. Useful for the next pub quiz.

Four.

But, pea brain, remember, you don't do pub quizzes now. Allow your mind to drift, if you want. Because you have sat down with the Lonely Planet you can read more about Italy. Think about the cypress trees, that heat, the bars, the streets, all the people continuing in all their various Italian lives, right now, even though you're not there to see it all, but sat here in the kitchen.

Five.

It's still not meal time but note the cat still demands food. All right. Keep your fur on, cat. Decide it's ok to disrupt the routine because, when it comes to it, routine doesn't solve anything. Fetch a pack from the box of Sheba Select Collection, slices in gravy – Jesus – when did she get so epicurean, and feed her. A fed cat is a happy cat. Except, she continues to prowl around, puzzled by the way thing are. And when she vomits up all her dinner, like she does, just – because – to prove a point or something, remember it's always your turn from now on to clean up after her. You can't pretend you hadn't seen it happen, like you used to, because that's not going to work, and the cat sure as hell isn't going to do it. So, go and fetch the cleaning stuff and get on with it.

Six

When you've done that, you can continue to ignore the juggling balls on top of the fridge. No-one, seriously, cares if you can do the five-ball cascade or not.

Seven.

Yes, ok, now, go outside for your permitted exercise. Hi trees. Hi outdoor air. How you doing? Sit on a bench and watch the same old guy who goes by every day to see what it's like to be his particular version of old. He has two sticks and seats himself down slowly on a nearby bench. Everybody else going by wears headphones, or jogs along, intent, apart from this ancient geezer. He looks around expectant, like it's a big event, this time outdoors, for him. He's dressed up for the occasion, with his jacket, his tie, and his old brown shoes polished to a glow, polished enough that when you see them, remember not to allow your heart to fracture one small bit. What does it matter that this guy polishes his shoes for this moment of his day when he goes out, but no-one speaks to him of course, because random conversations don't happen at the moment, and – was it mentioned – everyone is too damn busy doing their own thing.

Eight.
You can give him a small wave of your hand here. Note how he has to lever himself up off the bench with his sticks, to head off home in his especially clean and polished shoes. Maybe he too has a cat back home, or a dog, or a goldfish, or a house plant even, waiting for him. You can hope this. Maybe, anyway, he's fine. Maybe it's you that misses someone knowing how you're doing.

Nine.
Back home. You can search around for one of those luggage labels you bought when you were both planning that Italian holiday. The beige labels with that reinforced bit around the hole and white string attached to it. You can write a message on this label. And then why not carefully tie it around a jar of plum jam. The biggest jar, on the left hand side of the line of jars. Stroke the cat some more.

Ten.

When it's the right time, you may head outside for the usual exercise. Go on, put the jar of plum jam on that bench. Sit and watch and wait. You can hope the old guy will come pottering along at his usual sort of time and sit down in his usual sort of way. You can hope he will see the jar of jam and read the label that says 'This is for you.' He probably won't know that you wanted to write something else. How you wanted, really, to write a memo to yourself – it will pass, it will change, do not look back, look forward.

Eleven.

Now return home.

Twelve.

Greet the cat. Remind her it's not meal time yet. Pick up the juggling balls from the top of the fridge because – memory, focus, movement. Go.

Sketchbook
Jane McLaughlin

He says it is like Elysium. Whatever that might be.

City people come down in their carriages and go home with a bunch of bluebells or a basket of blackberries and think they have been in the country.

But that is not the way he is. He walks here. He says he has been walking here ever since he was a little boy and came here with his father, through the lanes and the streams, looking for nuts and mushrooms and pretty stones, and fishing tadpoles out of the brook. And always he carries his book and his pens, stopping often to look and to draw.

So when he comes to our gate I give him not just a cup of water but a handful of whatever is good at the time – a few sweet pea-pods or raspberries. His delight is like a child – well he is little more than a child, nineteen I think he told me.

Last summer when he passed Father was sitting in the orchard reading to Sarah and Lily. He drew Father with his white beard like a prophet, the girls kneeling either side of him. There was a house behind them but it did not look like our cottage.

He's not strong, looks thin and pale for a young man of his years and he suffers with his lungs. Mother died when he was thirteen he tells me, poor little man. But he strides along when he comes here, gazing up and around all the time as he goes and I would say he looks happy.

I think I know what kind of house he lives in. I have passed them when I have been up to the market with John in the cart. Tall sooty houses with fireplaces in every room. I do not go very often, too much noise and dirt, bad smells and bad air, and the cobblestones shake my bones.

So he walks down from the city, across the river, through Newington Butts, where they grow grapes in glasshouses and peaches for rich tables, and Walworth and at last into our pretty streams and hills. In the market gardens and cornfields the air is good.

I fear for him in the winter, but he still comes, wearing a big greatcoat with heavy capes, and still carrying his book and pens, still drawing.

In summer he draws the horse chestnut trees that grow like white and pink castles. Sometimes he shows his book to us; I do not know what to make of some of the drawings, they look scratchy and wild. I do not recognise the people or the places or understand some of the ugly beasts and strange images. But I admire the ones of trees; he has studied the shape and character of each of them. As if he was drawing portraits of people – there are trees you can see if you walk around here, trees that I know. And some of the pages in his book have pretty sketches of leaves and branches.

'There are such fine trees in this place. I want to know them, how they live and change through the seasons.'

Now it is June and we pick late into the evening, as long as the light lasts. Raspberries, strawberries, currants packed in baskets and boxes. Fine lettuces and radishes. As much as we can gather, because this is the time of year when we can make money to save for the winter, when there will be little more than cabbages and leeks.

Past here he's off again, sometimes back into the city, sometimes up through Peckham to Greenwich and the river. I tell him I think it must be very muddy and bare up there but:

'There are palaces along the banks, and a great shining river and tall ships going into the quays at Deptford.'

I see it in my mind's eye.

Mostly he comes on his own, but there is another man who comes along too, always drawing as well and talking twenty to the dozen. And then there was an older man with a big head and staring blue eyes who said he has seen angels in the trees.

Well I have seen angels too. I saw them after little Charlie died of the scarlet fever two winters ago.

Today I see him coming along the lane in his brown hat and light coat. It is warm and bright and the trees are full of their summer leaves.

He asks after Father and John and the children. I tell him they are out in the fruit bushes.

'I am moving to Kent very soon. The air will be better for my lungs. There are beautiful hills and woods there. But Dulwich will always be my first inspiration, where my eye first learnt to read the landscape and the way the day changes it from twilight to twilight.'

He takes a page from his book. It is the drawing of Father reading to the girls that he made last year. I thank him kindly. I can't read the writing on it. I will put it away to give to Sarah when she is older. Father never taught me to read, but I will make sure he teaches Sarah and Lily.

I give him a bunch of radishes: red, yellow, white, purple, washed with fresh water from the pump.

Again his face shows delight.

'Rainbow. Sunset.' he says and puts them in his pocket.

He walks away from the cottage. I watch him pass in and out of the light under the horse chestnut trees.

Before he reaches the end of the lane he stops and takes out his sketchbook.

He is drawing a tree.

A chaunce may wynne
            that by mischance was lost:

nett that houldes no greate,
                takes little fish;

In some thinges all,
        in all thinges none are croste,

Fewe all they neede,
        but none have all they wishe;

Unmedled joyes here
                        no man befall.

Who least hath some,
            who most hath never all.

Sir Thomas Wyatt's Cat
Elinor Brooks

After 'They Flee From Me' by Sir Thomas Wyatt

He seeks me out, that sometime did me flee
With white-sock foot, trotting the empty alley.
I have seen him moving fearful, lame
That now is tame and comes direct to me
Nosing my outstretched hand quite casually
For fish-skins, fat or ham, and now he struts abroad
Purring his loud contentment to the road.

179cm
C L Hearnden

We always think we are done growing.
That, that's it.
That, right now, the us that's breathing,
the *I think therefore I am*
is all that we are.

It is only on looking back that we see any grow lines at all. But if,
like a child, we run back to the wall of measurements
the one with those little centimetre markings,
too hungry for tallness for newness for biggerness,
we will be disappointed. Stuck
bluntly under that etching in the wall; A lead ceiling.

We'll sulk off into the rest of our life, then one sudden day –
we are back;
In our childhood home, towering over every etching of our
past self.
Standing overgrown in the shards
of that line roof that once limited us.

Roots
Patience Mackarness

Where he was born, the earth was stony. Nodules of broken flint made his toes bleed. He was never going to stay.

Beneath his college town, the soil is clay-based and dense. He considers settling, for he's been happy here; he's been excited by learning, has fallen in love and out of it, watched the flowering of his limbs and his imagination. He's already sunk up to his knees when winter rains saturate the land and floodwater spreads over the fields. He feels dragged down, trapped. He says *Not here*.

He spends years in a distant place, a small hot island simmering with wealth and optimism, whose name means 'Two Seas'. Legend tells of another, sweeter sea beneath the salt ocean, feeding ancient springs that made the island fertile and its people prosperous. In that crumbly earth, he's both grounded and free. Money loosens everything. He addresses conferences and board directors about the benefits of endless growth.

He marries and moves back home, to a select neighbourhood on a hill near the golf club. His roots are thick and long, but his pleasure in their reach is subtly reduced. His wife, however, is happy. She purrs as she assures him *size does matter*.

By the time he knows he's in the wrong place, he's too deeply anchored. His toes graze tiny threads of mycelium. He used to make corporate jokes about mushrooms, *keep them in the dark and feed them on shit, you'll never go far wrong!* Now he envies them their wordless communication, their certainty of belonging. He starts to hate the golf club.

He's old. Wives and children have left him. It's too late to move on, his strength has leaked away, along with his memory and bladder control.

He's forgotten that his roots have continued to push downward. They're thinner, and their growth is slower, but they have their own logic, and can find lost ways, seek out hidden paths below. In darkness, they find the other, sweeter, sea.

New Orleans to Vancouver: a Railway Journey
Katie Margaret Hall

Eighty-eight hours, three thousand miles, four Amtrak trains
trailer homes line up on the wrong side of the tracks
Sunset Limited, Starlight Coast, Amtrak Cascades
red dusk falls over glass skyscrapers

trailer homes line up on the wrong side of the tracks
the constant horn alerts level crossing drivers of our approach
red dusk falls over glass skyscrapers
evergreens turn to dust

the constant horn alerts level crossing drivers of our approach
on open plains, livestock graze free range
evergreens turn to dust
Mexico a stone's throw over a brown metal fence

on open plains, livestock graze free range
Joshua trees stand to attention
Mexico a stone's throw over a brown metal fence
lightning forks over the Arizona sunset

Joshua trees stand to attention
crows surround a lifeless cow
lightning forks over the Arizona sunset
palm trees wait for our arrival

crows surround a lifeless cow
breakers roll in over forgotten footprints
palm trees ignore our departure
tandem dolphins swim past the window

breakers roll in over forgotten footprints
impossible cliffs defend gold rush memories
tandem dolphins swim past the window
mists cloak the pacific crest trail, white-washing their peaks

impossible cliffs defend gold rush memories
redwoods become evergreen
mists blanket sea-level trails, white-washing the horizon
a creek runs alongside, racing us

redwoods become evergreen
Sunset Limited, Starlight Coast, Amtrak Cascades
a creek runs alongside, racing us
eighty-eight hours, three thousand miles, four train journeys.

Sirius
Jane Aldous

Poor wee dug, slug, mutt, kicked and starved,
scarred with dog-ends, as lost as the man beside him –
is there the ghost of a wolf under his skin?

Wolves: what if we could hear their voices reverberating
through thirty-thousand years of permafrost
heads thrown back, tongues quivering, bloodied jowls
wide open, ravens calling overhead?

And what if howls came back through time,
telling of slavering descendants, trapped,

turning spit-roast pigs, caged for meat,
bred beyond all recognition,

would they still be tempted by
fire-charred bones, and cower willingly at human feet?
Hard to recognise but here, in those unreadable eyes,

in the furious body of a terrier shaking against his, a dog-wolf,
who will choose to be loved and fed, to be with
this man, wherever he is.